AND THE
JURASSIC PORTAL

WRITTEN & ILLUSTRATED BY FRANCO

STONE ARCH BOOKS
a capstone imprint

Dino-Mike! is published by
Stone Arch Books,
a Capstone imprint
1710 Roe Crest Drive
North Mankato, Minnesota 56003
www.capstoneyoungreader.com

Cataloging-in-Publication Data is available on
the Library of Congress website.

ISBN: 978-1-4342-9630-6 (library hardcover)
ISBN: 978-1-4965-0168-4 (eBook)
ISBN: 978-1-4342-9634-4 (paperback)

Summary: Dino-Mike finds a portal to the Jurassic
Age in this chapter book adventure!

Printed in Canada
042015   008825FRF15

CONTENTS

Young Mike Evans travels the world with his dino-hunting dad. From the Jurassic Coast in Great Britain to the Liaoning Province in China, young Dino-Mike has been there, *dug* that!

When his dad is dusting fossils, Mike's boning up on his own dino skills — only he's finding the real deal. A live T. rex egg! A portal to the Jurassic period!! An undersea dinosaur sanctuary!!!

Prepare yourself for another wild and wacky Dino-Mike adventure, which nobody will ever believe . . .

Chapter 1
TIME WARP

"I'm GLOWING!" Mike screamed.

He was indeed glowing . . . and falling! FAST! Mike wasn't sure where he'd eventually land, but that thought didn't make him panic. He was more concerned about the strange radioactive glow. Dr. Broome told him this might happen, but it still didn't seem safe.

Glowing in the dark can't be good for you. It's just not normal, Mike worried. *I may never get a good night's sleep again!*

Suddenly, there was a rush of air, and then **THUD!** Dino-Mike hit the ground.

"Uhn . . ." Mike groaned in pain.

After a moment, Dino-Mike lifted his head and looked down at his hands. They were still glowing!

"How do I shut this off?" Mike exclaimed. He knew any nearby animals would be attracted to the strange light.

Mike stood and brushed dirt from his Dino Jacket. The high-tech hoodie — the best-ever present from his dad — had helped him once again. The Dino Jacket's specially designed fabric had cushioned his fall and saved him from breaking bones . . . or worse.

Mike's glowing skin soon returned to normal, but his problems weren't over.

Mike needed to find his dino-hunting sidekick, Shannon. He'd agreed to travel back in time because her mad-scientist father, Dr. Broome, needed help.

Dino-Mike reached inside his hoodie and pulled out a small gadget. The high-tech device looked like a TV remote control. In fact, it *was* a TV remote control! Dr. Broome had transformed the device into Mike's life raft, which he called a Return Remote.

When Mike located Shannon, he needed to return to this spot and click the device's rewind button. That would send them back to the present day.

Priority number one, Mike thought, *find Shannon.*

Mike scanned his surroundings. He still didn't know where he was located or even what time period he was in. However, being the son of a famous paleontologist, Dino-Mike did know a lot about dinosaurs and their environments.

Mike observed the surrounding plants and rocks. "The late Jurassic .," he concluded. "Or maybe the early Cretaceous period. There's only one way to know for sure —"

CRUNNNNNNNNNNNNNCH!

Suddenly, Dino-Mike heard a loud crunching noise in the nearby forest. Whatever was behind those trees would be Mike's clue to his location. But he didn't need to know that badly!

Dino-Mike followed a nearby trail away from the sound. Soon, he stopped and pulled a journal from the inside pocket of his Dino Jacket.

The journal didn't belong to him. It belonged to his worst enemy . . .

"Jurassic Jeff," Mike growled.

Jurassic Jeff had one evil goal: to repopulate present-day Earth with dinosaurs. He'd stop at nothing to accomplish this fearsome feat.

Oh, and he just happened to be Shannon's big brother! Crazy, right?

On his last big adventure, Dino-Mike managed to secure Jeff's journal. Mike hoped it would reveal Jeff's secret plans.

Paging through the journal, Mike found maps. Landmarks on one map seemed to match Mike's location!

FWOOOOSH!

A sudden wind flipped the pages of the journal.

FWOOOOSH!

The wind came again, hot and humid like the breath of a . . .

Dino-Mike pocketed the journal and spun around. He was nose to horn with an angry dinosaur.

"Triceratops!" Mike exclaimed.

Chapter 2
CHARGE!

"A triple threat!" Mike screamed.

Mike quickly turned and sprinted away from the three-horned beast. The triceratops was hot on his trail.

Mike knew he could never outrun a triceratops. His extreme knowledge of dinos told Mike that they could run like rhinos — thirty miles per hour!

Thinking fast, Mike stopped and spun toward the triceratops. He grabbed his hood and flipped it onto his head.

"DINO-MIKE!" he screamed.

ROOOOAAAAAAAARRRRR!

The sound of a T. rex roar blasted from speakers inside his Dino Jacket.

That should scare him, thought Mike.

The beast grunted and snorted and his eyes turned red with rage.

"Uh-oh," said Mike. In his panic, he'd forgotten that triceratops, unlike most dinosaurs, often defended themselves from T. rex attacks.

The triceratops thrashed, snorted again, and kicked up dirt. Then the beast charged at Dino-Mike like a raging bull.

"Move!" shouted a nearby voice.

A split-second later, a figure tackled Mike out of the triceratops's path. Again, Dino-Mike hit the ground with a **THUD!**

"Ugh," Mike said, picking himself up off the ground. "What's the big idea?"

"You can thank me later," said the redheaded girl standing next to him.

"SHANNON!" Mike exclaimed, recognizing his dino-hunting sidekick. "I'm so glad to see you —"

"Less talk," Shannon interrupted, "more running!"

SMASH! CRASH!

The angry triceratops had turned around. It was smashing and crashing through the trees toward the duo.

"Follow me!" cried Shannon. She turned and headed straight into a mess of thick plants and vines.

"We'll never outrun him in here," shouted Mike.

"We don't need to," Shannon replied.

Breaking through the vines, Dino-Mike spotted the edge of a cliff only a few yards away. The cliff dropped more than a hundred feet to a valley below!

"We're trapped!" Mike told Shannon as the triceratops edged them closer to the cliff. "Why did you lead us here?"

Shannon grabbed Mike's wrist. "Sorry," she explained, "I'm just thinking on the fly!"

Then Shannon leaped over the cliff, pulling Dino-Mike along with her.

"AHH!" Mike screamed as they plummeted toward the ground below.

Chapter 3
FREE FALL

"Hey!" screamed Mike. "I thought you were my dino-hunting sidekick. Shouldn't I know about big decisions, like jumping off a cliff?"

"You're right," said Shannon. "From now on, I'll tell you everything."

As they fell, Shannon grabbed the drawstrings of Dino-Mike's hoodie.

"FYI," she told Mike, "I'm going to pull these."

"Wait —!" shouted Dino-Mike.

But Shannon had already pulled the strings. When she did, a pair of wings sprouted from under Mike's arms!

FWOOSH! For a moment, Mike and Shannon glided above the ground.

"How did you know my Dino Jacket had wings?" Mike asked Shannon.

"Your hoodie has all kinds of dinosaur powers," Shannon replied. "I just figured it had a pterodactyl mode."

"Did you also assume I could fly it?" asked Dino-Mike.

Mike flapped his wings frantically, and soon the duo was plummeting toward the ground again.

Just then, an alarm sounded, and the Dino Jacket puffed up like a balloon!

BEEP! BEEP! BEEP!

"What's that noise?" asked Shannon.

"I don't know," Mike replied. "The Dino Jacket must have some kind of emergency safety mode!"

Dino-Mike and Shannon floated slowly toward the valley below. When they hit the ground, the jacket bounced several times like a giant basketball.

Finally they came to a stop. The Dino Jacket quickly deflated back to its original size and shape.

"So, what are you doing here?" Shannon said, ignoring the fact that they'd almost died.

"Your father sent me to find you," replied Mike.

"My father?" asked Shannon. "Did he give you a Return Remote?"

"Yes," said Mike, reaching into his Dino Jacket and revealing the high-tech device. "It's right here."

"OH MY GOSH! Do you know what this means?" Shannon exclaimed.

"It means we can get out of here," answered Dino-Mike. He grabbed Shannon's arm and started pulling her along a nearby trail.

"Wait!" said Shannon. "We can't. Not yet, anyway."

"Why?" asked Mike, puzzled.

Shannon hesitated and then said, "First, we need to find Jeff."

Dino-Mike gritted his teeth, and his face turned redder than a tomato.

"JURASSIC JEFF!" Mike shouted, sweat and steam rising from his forehead. "My. Worst. Enemy."

"Don't forget, Mike," said Shannon, "he's also my brother."

"A real brother wouldn't kidnap his sister and drag her to the Jurassic Age!" Mike shot back.

"First," Shannon began, "this isn't the Jurassic Age. It's the Cretaceous period. Any dino-hunter would know that!"

"D'oh!" Mike exclaimed.

"Second," Shannon continued, "Jeff didn't kidnap me. I chose to come back in time with him."

"You're kidding, right?" said Mike.

"You're not going to believe me, Mike, but we have a much bigger problem than my brother!" Shannon explained.

"What could possibly be worse than Jurassic Jeff?" shouted Mike.

"MOM!" Shannon exclaimed.

"What are you talking about?" Dino-Mike demanded.

"For years, Jeff has tried to bring one or two dinosaurs back to the present day," Shannon explained. "But MOM is trying to bring back thousands!"

"THOUSANDS!" Mike repeated.

"That's what I've been trying to tell you, Mike," said Shannon. "Jeff might be evil minded, but MOM is a mastermind."

"But why?" asked Dino-Mike.

"She's just programmed that way, I guess," Shannon suggested.

"How do we stop her?" said Mike.

"You're not going to like my answer," Shannon began. "But we're going to have to work with Jurassic Jeff!"

"Uh-uh," said Mike, shaking his head furiously. "No way."

"Come on, Mike," Shannon pleaded. "It could be our only chance. Jurassic Jeff's the only one who knows how to push MOM's buttons."

"How can we trust him?" asked Dino-Mike. He thought back to many of Jeff's other adventures. Just weeks ago, the evil teenager had released a T. rex onto the streets of New York City! That event could have ended in disaster.

"I can't lie to you," replied Shannon. "Jeff hasn't changed. But he knows that MOM's plan goes too far. Not even he'll be safe from thousands of dinosaurs."

"Maybe you're right," said Mike.

"Besides," Shannon continued, "what other choice do we have? Right now, Jeff is the lesser of two evils. What do you say? Are you ready to take a leap of faith with me, old pal?"

"Um, didn't I already do that?" Mike replied, pointing to the nearby cliff.

The duo laughed.

Then Mike stepped toward Shannon and extended his hand.

"Okay," he said. "We'll work with Jeff until your mom is captured . . . but don't ask me to like it."

Shannon smiled and then reached out and shook Dino-Mike's hand.

"Deal!" she said.

"DINO-MIKE!" they both exclaimed.

Chapter 4

FAMILY TREE

Following Jurassic Jeff's journal, Dino-Mike and Shannon made their way across the narrow valley. Finally, they reached a small, dense forest.

"Shh," Shannon shushed Dino-Mike. "Stay quiet and pay attention!" She kneeled down and studied a footprint in the dirt.

"A dinosaur?" asked Mike.

Dino-Mike stepped forward for a closer look. "What species?" he wondered. "Diplodocus? Pentaceratops?"

Shannon started to giggle.

"What?" questioned Mike. "Do you know what kind of track that is?"

WHUMP!

Mike was suddenly tackled to the ground.

"A Jurassic Jeff track!" Shannon said, letting out a laugh.

Mike tried to move, but Jurassic Jeff had him pinned to the ground. "Get off of me!" shouted Dino-Mike, struggling to get free.

Finally Jeff stood and turned to Shannon. "What is he doing here?"

"Trying to help you!" said Dino-Mike, standing and dusting off his Dino Jacket.

"What are you talking about?" asked Jeff. "How are *you* going to help *me*?!"

"It's true," Shannon explained to her brother. "Dad sent him to find us."

"Again, what are you talking about?" asked Jeff. "How did he send him right to where we were? Dad must have figured out how to time target!"

"He sent me because he thought you kidnapped Shannon," said Mike.

"Why would he think that?" said Jeff.

"Really?" said Shannon. "You haven't exactly been trustworthy in the past."

"Oh," said Jeff. "When you put it that way, I might have thought that too. But still, I guess it says a lot that Dad sent him. Means he really trusts you, Mike."

Dino-Mike felt the compliment. Jeff had given him a lot of trouble in the past (he was Mike's worst enemy, after all!), but he seemed like he wanted to be a better person.

"Thanks," Mike said.

Shannon spoke up again. "Dad doesn't know about MOM."

"Makes sense," said Jeff. "If he did, he probably wouldn't have sent Mike."

How bad can their mother be? thought Mike. He knew he'd probably find out soon enough!

Jeff turned to go back into the forest and started down a narrow path.

"If we're going to track MOM, we better get going!" he said, leading the way. "Oh, and welcome to the expedition, Mike. Don't get your hopes up about ever returning home."

"Thanks," said Mike. He knew Jeff's kindness couldn't last long.

Chapter 5
CAVE MOM

A short while later, the group peered at the entrance of a cave.

"Do you think MOM's in there?" asked Shannon.

They had traveled an hour through dense leaves, vines, and branches. It was the hardest trek through any stretch of forest Dino-Mike had ever made.

"If she isn't, she will be soon." Jeff moved behind a nearby tree to get a better look at the cave. "The equipment she needs is stored in that cave."

"Unless she's already been here and is back out gathering herds of dinosaurs," Shannon suggested.

"Um . . ." Mike interrupted. "Not to sound like I don't know what you guys are talking about, but what are you talking about?!"

"If you haven't figured it out yet, Jeff is very tech savvy. He developed some equipment that would enhance the portal process," explained Shannon.

"What does that mean?" asked Mike.

"It means that I think I figured out a way to make the time portal work on a large scale," said Jeff, still trying to get a better look into the cave.

"Large scale," repeated Mike. "Does he mean —?"

"If MOM accesses the portal with the equipment Jeff developed, she might be able to transport a whole bunch of dinosaurs at once," confirmed Shannon.

"That was before I, you know, became good," Jeff reminded them. "The last T. rex I brought back was my phase-one experiment. I knew that if I could transport one dinosaur directly to a site, I had the ability to transport a whole bunch of them at once."

"So it's not just a possibility. If she gets that equipment, it's definite! She'll be able to bring thousands of dinosaurs to the present day?" asked Mike.

"Yeah," said Jeff. "Pretty much."

"Are you serious?!" exclaimed Mike.

Mike looked at Shannon. It was up to them to think of a plan. Mike thought about the situation.

If Jeff and Shannon's mom needed that equipment, the simplest solution would be to keep her from using it. Mike carefully looked at the cave entrance. Above the mouth of the cave was a pile of rocks that must have tumbled down from farther up the hillside. There was a tree blocking their path. Otherwise, the rocks would have fallen and possibly covered the opening to the cave.

Mike started
climbing a tree faster
than a monkey.

FWIP! FWIP!

Raptor claws in
Mike's sleeves dug into
the bark of the tree,
making his climb a
breeze.

Before Shannon
could shout out for him
to stop, he was already
at the top of the tree.

Swinging from tree to tree, Mike made it to the space just above the cave entrance. Then suddenly, Mike froze.

In front of him was a family of triceratops — a mother and two little ones. Based on his last encounter, Dino-Mike wasn't excited to see them!

The mother was huge, as you would expect a dinosaur would be. The young triceratops were roughly the size of rhinoceroses, which meant they were still a lot bigger than Dino-Mike was. And, like any good camper, he knew not to mess with a mother and her cubs.

That gave Dino-Mike an idea!

Dino-Mike approached the grazing triceratops cautiously. At first, the family of triceratops completely ignored him. Obviously, these triceratops were not even remotely related to the triceratops he had met at the landing point, or they would have chased him the minute he came above the rise.

Mike stood tall and pulled on the drawstrings of his hoodie. Two streams of water blasted out of the drawstring holes and hit the mother triceratops on the butt!

SPA-LOOOOOOOOOOSH!

The mother triceratops reacted as if a swarm of bees, rather than a cool stream of water, had hit her. She spotted Mike and let out a **ROOOOAR!**

The triceratops turned toward him and, along with her babies, started running right at Mike.

Okay, maybe this was a mistake, thought Mike.

Dino-Mike ran for the rocks and trees. He had to time this plan just right. Mike stepped up on the rocks, ran over them while trying not to lose his footing, and leaped, barely missing the tree holding up the rocks.

As he jumped, Mike looked back to see if his plan had worked. Sure enough, the mother triceratops had smashed into the tree, splintering it to pieces.

In doing so, the rocks that were being held back started to give way. The triceratops mom and her babies scrambled off the large pile of rocks to safety before the rocks fell over the cliff.

Mike watched all this happen as his Dino Jacket came to his rescue once again. He heard the distinct sound of air rushing through the jacket's vents. The jacket inflated to the size of a large balloon, and Mike gently floated to the tree line where Shannon and Jeff waited.

As he landed, the large rocks that had been dislodged were crashing down and covering the entrance to the cave.

Jeff and Shannon came out from behind the trees. Mike smiled as he surveyed his handiwork.

"See? No more worries," said Mike as his jacket deflated back to normal size. "Your mom is trapped in there. Now we can go back to the future, tell your dad, and bring back some help."

"I don't know," said Jeff. "That's not going to hold MOM."

"I think you're right," said Shannon. "And now MOM knows we're here!"

Mike was in total disbelief. "What is the matter with you guys? Your mother is never going to get out of there without help. Those rocks weigh a ton!"

"My mother?" asked Jeff.

"What makes you think our mother is in the cave?" asked Shannon.

"Because you said your mom was in there," Mike screamed.

"No. We said *MOM* was in there," explained Jeff.

"What's the difference?" asked Mike.

Suddenly, there was a loud **CRACK!**

The group turned in time to see the
pile of rocks covering the entrance to the
cave explode outward.

SMAAASSSSSSSSSSSH!!!

Suddenly, a large mechanical robot emerged from the cave. It loomed over the group. Mike couldn't believe what he was looking at. The robot was lifting the largest boulder — the one that Mike couldn't even budge at the top of the ridge — over its head.

Shannon said, *"That's* MOM!"

Chapter 6

ROCK AND ROLL

"Your mom's a ROBOT?!" asked Mike, still confused.

The robot — which did not look anything like a mom — lifted another boulder over its head. Then the mechanical menace tossed the huge rock to the ground with all its might.

WHAM-O!

Dino-Mike gulped in fright.

"No! That's not our mother!" Shannon explained. "Our mother passed away when we were young."

"That's MOM!" offered Jeff.

"Why do you have a MOM?" asked Mike, realizing that sounded totally ridiculous. "I mean, a robot named MOM?"

"MOM stands for Maintenance Operations Machine," Jeff replied.

"It was a maintenance robot our dad retrofitted to watch over us whenever we were here in the past," said Shannon as they continued to watch the robot work to clear itself from the rubble.

"You mean your dad made you a robot nanny that would protect you in case you got attacked by a T. rex?" asked Dino-Mike.

"Something like that. But me being me, I reprogrammed it," offered Jeff.

"To help you bring dinosaurs to the future?" asked Mike. Things were starting to make sense now.

"I kind of had a one-track mind when it came to dinosaurs," said Jeff. "I programmed MOM to bring back one dinosaur, but somehow the program got stuck on repeat. The robot won't stop now until it brings all of them back."

"So shut it down!" Mike shouted.

"I can't. I overrode the failsafe switch, so no one could turn it off. It won't stop until it accomplishes its task — until present-day Earth is overrun by dinosaurs," said Jeff, starting to panic.

"So then we destroy it!" said Mike.

THUD!

A large boulder landed just inches away from the trio.

"That won't be easy!" said Shannon.

"It's superstrong and programmed to do two things," Jeff started. "Bring dinosaurs back to our time and —"

Shannon pushed both her brother and Mike down to the ground as another rock landed, barely missing them.

WHAM!

From the ground, they watched as the MOM robot grabbed another rock and hoisted the boulder over its head.

"What's the second thing?" asked Mike, afraid of the answer.

"Stop anyone who's trying to prevent it from bringing dinosaurs to our time," said Jeff.

They were stuck. All three of them were on the ground as the MOM robot approached. There was no way to get out of the way.

MOM was going to drop the rock right on top of them.

Mike held his breath. "Could this be the end of Dino-Mike?" he muttered.

Chapter 7

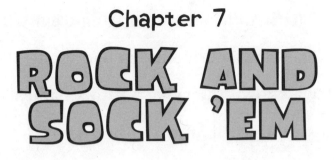

ROCK AND SOCK 'EM

CLANG!

It was the sudden and horrible sound of metal being hit by something big. The crunching and scraping sound of metal echoed throughout the forest.

They were saved! Mike watched as the triceratops smashed into the side of MOM. The robot toppled over.

The boulder it was holding went with it. The mother triceratops had made its way down the ridge with its babies. Apparently still angry with Mike for squirting it with water, it rammed into the side of the MOM robot.

Without thinking, Mike jumped up and let out a "HOORAY!" He was so relieved not to be crushed under a rock hurled by a robot. The sound of his rejoicing caught the attention of the triceratops. It turned toward him, Shannon, and Jeff.

"Uh-oh," said Shannon. "I don't think you should have done that."

The two small triceratops ran toward them. Luckily, the mother triceratops turned its attention back to MOM.

"We just traded being squashed by a rock for being trampled by dinosaurs!" said Jeff. "RUN!"

Mike, Shannon, and Jeff were mere steps ahead of the rushing triceratops!

"What else do you have in that Dino Jacket of yours, Mike?" asked Shannon.

Mike turned as Jeff and Shannon kept running. As he turned, he flipped his hood over his head. The T. rex eyes lit up like fireworks, flooding the area with light and blinding the triceratops.

The T. rex roar bellowed from the speakers of the hoodie. The two triceratops were caught by surprise. Their thundering footsteps suddenly changed to scrambling steps as they tried to get out of the way.

The roar was deafening and, although it scared away the younger triceratops, it also attracted attention Mike didn't want. After his T. rex roar faded, Mike heard a different kind of pounding footsteps.

He looked up to see MOM heading straight for him. The robot was almost on top of him. The only thing he could think to do as the robot reached for him was to jump up in the air.

His jacket quickly ballooned out like a round ball. MOM grabbed him in his puffy-jacket state, lifted him higher into the air, and squeezed.

It worked! Mike felt uncomfortable as MOM squeezed, but he wasn't getting crushed. Unfortunately, the squeezing caused the Return Remote to pop out of his jacket and fall to the ground. Mike could only look on helplessly as it fell.

He saw something else, though. The mother triceratops was back and headed straight for MOM.

As it charged, it crushed the Return Remote under its foot!

SMASH!

The triceratops smashed its horned head into the body of the robot. The clash knocked Mike loose from the robot's grip. He floated gently back to the ground.

As his jacket deflated, Jeff and Shannon ran up to him. They helped move Dino-Mike out of the way of the fighting robot and dinosaur.

"The Return Remote!" said Mike, pointing at the shattered device.

"What are we going to do?" asked Shannon.

"MOM's the answer," said Jeff. "Its internal return function is the only way we'll get back!"

"So, let me get this straight," Mike began. "We need to destroy the robot in order to save present-day Earth. But, if we destroy the robot, we're stuck here?!"

"Correct," answered Jurassic Jeff.

"Well, that's just great," said Mike.

Meanwhile, MOM had given its full attention to the triceratops. It clamped one hand down on the main horn of the dinosaur. This stopped the dinosaur from doing any more damage.

In fact, it stopped the dinosaur from doing anything at all. By holding on to its horn, MOM was able to drag the triceratops around like a dog on a leash.

"Uh-oh," said Jeff.

They all knew that having the dinosaur under control meant that MOM would be coming after them next.

"What do we do, Jeff?" asked Shannon.

"How should I know? I didn't build it!" said Jeff.

Mike couldn't think of a way out either. He decided to act, still not fully sure of what he was going to do.

He started running at the robot. As he reached the robot's legs, Mike reached out his arms as if to climb it like he would a tree. Sure enough, his raptor claws sprung out of his sleeves.

FWIP! FWIP!

Mike used the claws to dig into the robot's metal legs. He started to climb.

"What are you doing?" said Shannon.

"Jeff, is the central processor in the head?" yelled down Mike.

"Yes, but —" replied Jeff, but then he thought about what Mike just asked. "If we could somehow separate MOM's head from the rest of the body, it will be like unplugging it. MOM would just shut off, and we could probably still use the internal Return Remote housed in its body to get us home!"

They watched helplessly as Mike scrambled to the top of MOM. He held on tight and positioned himself behind MOM's head.

The robot released the triceratops and started swatting at Mike like a fly. Dino-Mike zigged and zagged, avoiding the mechanical menace's metal arms. Mike knew he didn't have much time.

At the same time, Shannon searched for a way to stop the triceratops and her babies. Suddenly, she noticed all of the vines that had wrapped themselves around the tall trees.

"I've got an idea! Help me gather these vines!" she yelled over at Jeff.

MOM spotted Shannon and Jeff and began to move toward them. Mike couldn't let the robot just go after them. He took off his Dino Jacket and wrapped it around the robot's head, blinding it.

Mike needed to shut down the robot, but to do that he would have to separate the head from the body.

He looked in the hood of his Dino Jacket. The inside of the hoodie was lined with an array of buttons. Mike quickly found the button he needed.

Mike pushed the button, and the jacket began to inflate to the size of a large balloon. Being wrapped around the robot's head, the jacket started to lift the whole robot off the ground.

Mike held on tight.

Then MOM suddenly stopped with a jerk. Jeff and Shannon had tied the robot to the ground with vines!

With a loud **CREAK!**, the robot's head started separating from its body.

MOM's head, wrapped in the Dino Jacket, lifted into the air along with a string of wires and metal from the inside of the robot. When the last of the wiring ripped from the body of the robot, the forest immediately went quiet.

"It worked!" shouted Dino-Mike.

Just then, Mike looked down to see Jeff and Shannon desperately trying to get his attention. Something was wrong. They were pointing above him.

Dino-Mike looked up and couldn't believe it. His Dino Jacket, zipped up around the head of the robot, was shooting into the air like a rocket!

Mike's mouth dropped open with shock as he watched it. The jacket must have calculated for the entire weight of the robot, but when the head was dislodged, it had not made any corrections. It thought it was still carrying the entire robot body.

Mike watched as the jacket and the robot head continued up into the sky and then vanished from sight.

Dino-Mike didn't have time to be angry. The headless robot swayed back and forth, ready to tip at any moment.

"TIMBER!" cried Dino-Mike, holding tightly to the falling robot.

CRAAAAASSHHHH!!!

The MOM robot hit the dirt, and the ground shook like a violent earthquake. A cloud of thick dust rose into the air.

Shannon and Jeff shielded their eyes. They couldn't see their friend through the dust and debris.

Then a figure emerged from the dust cloud, coughing and spitting. "Looks like we scared away the triceratops," said Mike, dusting himself off.

"DINO-MIKE!" Shannon and Jeff exclaimed.

Chapter 8

STUCK

"We're stuck here," said Jeff as he climbed down from the robot body.

Jeff explained how the Return Remote components had been ripped out of the body when the head was separated. Somewhere in that mess of spaghetti wire Mike watched float away was their ticket home.

"At the rate that thing was going, the head probably shot right into outer space," finished Jeff as his boots hit the ground next to Mike and Shannon.

"I can't believe my Dino Jacket is gone," said Mike. "It was a present from my dad, and now . . . it's lost forever."

Shannon put her hand on Mike's shoulder to comfort him. "You saved our lives. You're a hero," said Shannon.

She's right, thought Mike. *As long as we're okay, the jacket doesn't matter.*

With the robot destroyed, there was little hope of getting back home. Mike started throwing out ideas.

"We could just wait for your dad to send someone back for us!" said Mike.

"True, but that could take years," said Shannon. "Time travel is never exact, because you're dealing with time. Dad will send someone back, but for us to see them arrive, it could be minutes or years or . . . never."

"The only way we can get back is with something that has already traveled forward in time through the portal," explained Jeff.

"Easy!" said Mike. "You guys have already done that."

"Not so easy," said Jeff. "For some reason it doesn't work with people. That's why we need the Return Remotes. My dad was the one who figured out how time travel works. I'm pretty smart when it comes to tech stuff and hardware, but time travel is way out of my league.

"When Dad first developed all this, he tried lots of different things. He sent objects back and forth through time to see what worked and what didn't before deciding it was safe enough to try it on the first human being . . . himself."

"What kind of things?" asked Mike.

"He told us he tried everything: tools, food, plants, and goldfish. You name it, he probably sent it here," said Shannon.

"Great! We find one of those things he sent back, and we're good to go, right?" said a hopeful Mike.

"Nope. Everything he sent, he brought back again. He didn't want to accidentally leave something from our time that someone would eventually discover through the ages," said Jeff.

"Great! So we're stuck millions of years in the past with a deranged MOM robot and dinosaurs everywhere we turn," shouted Mike, defeated.

Everyone went silent. Mike let out a sigh and sat down on the nearest rock. He would never see his dad again.

Funny, Mike thought. *Dad would love this place.*

Dino-Mike stared at the ground. There were reminders all around that dinosaurs roamed the planet freely. He immediately recognized a fresh dinosaur footprint on the ground in front of him.

It was the footprint of a fully grown T. rex! It reminded him of the one his father and a team of paleontologists had unearthed just a few months earlier.

That was the day he met Shannon.

"Wait a minute!" said Mike, standing up and grabbing Shannon by the shoulders. "The T. rex! *Our* T. rex — the one we named Samantha! Tell me you brought her here!"

Shannon's eyes went wide.

"Yes!" she said.

Jeff knew exactly what they were talking about. "You and Dad brought her back here?" he asked Shannon.

"Yes!" said Shannon. She smiled for a moment but then stopped. "But how are we going to find her?"

Mike pulled out a journal from his back pocket. "With this!"

"My journal!" said Jeff. "Where did you get that?"

"From your room on the *Atlantica* submarine," replied Mike slowly, thinking Jeff was going to be angry that he had gone through his stuff.

Jeff moved in on Mike. For a split second, Mike thought Jeff was going to attack him. But Jeff hugged him instead. Mike was shocked.

"Dude!" said Jeff, continuing the hug. "I am so happy you brought that along!"

Chapter 9

OLD FRIENDS

Mike was getting tired of sneaking around. But if they could pull off this plan, they would all get home.

They were close to the landing site, just next to the nest of a mother T. rex and her babies. This wasn't just any T. rex, either. It was Samantha. Mike had run into her on earlier dino adventures!

Mike, Shannon, and Jeff looked at the T. rex and her four babies, which had grown a couple of feet since the last time Mike saw them. They were frolicking and playing around her like a litter of new puppies.

Since the babies were born in New York City, only the mother T. rex had gone forward in time. Only she could trigger the portal. They were going to take one of the babies and lure the mother to the landing site in hopes that she would activate the portal.

The plan was easy. It was a very dangerous plan but a simple one.

"I'm not too sure about this," said Shannon.

"Me neither. But if we want a chance of getting back rather than waiting to see if we get rescued, I say we take the risk," whispered Jeff.

"It's dangerous," said Shannon.

"This won't be the first time today that we've done something dangerous," whispered Mike.

Shannon gave him a look that said both "Yes, you're right" and "I can't believe this is about to happen."

"Okay," she finally said. "How are we going to do this?"

"Without the Dino Jacket, it's going to be difficult. If two of us distract the mother and one of us swoops in and grabs a baby, with any luck she'll chase us. We can lead her right back to the landing site," said Mike.

"I don't think calling them babies is appropriate. Those things are like six feet long," said Jeff.

"Since Jeff and I have the most experience with larger dinosaurs, we'll get the mother's attention. You get in and try for one of the kids," said Shannon.

"I really wish we had a can of Dad's knockout spray right now," said Jeff.

Mike smiled as he remembered the minty taste of the knockout spray. He wished they had one right now too. *It would make things so much easier,* he thought.

Mike lifted the makeshift leash they had made out of vines for one of the baby T. rex. He looked at Shannon and Jeff. They nodded at each other and started putting their plan into action.

Mike waited a few minutes as Shannon and Jeff moved through the trees. Then he made his way to

the opposite end of the open field where the T. rex were. He waited for the right time.

From the other side of the field he heard Jeff's voice. "Hey, you big old T. rex!"

BOOOOM! BOOOOM!

Mike could hear the booming footsteps of the mother T. rex as she moved away. Mike looked out and saw Jeff and Shannon waving to try to capture the dinosaur's attention.

"Come on! We're over here! Chase us!" Shannon called out.

The T. rex moved toward their direction. Jeff and Shannon didn't wait around any longer and started running into the forest.

Mike bolted out of the trees and sprinted straight for one of the baby T. rex.

Dino-Mike chose the closest one, slipped the leash around its neck, and immediately started running.

"I got one! I got one!" he yelled out, so that Jeff and Shannon would know to start heading for the landing site.

Mike was suddenly jerked back, and he almost fell as the leashed T. rex stood fast. Mike quickly got back to his feet and tugged on the leash. The T. rex wouldn't budge.

Now it had caught the attention of the other three kid T. rex. Mike was pulling with all his might, but the T. rex remained stubborn.

The four T. rex began playing and frolicking with each other. One of them was even chewing on the makeshift leash.

"No," whispered Mike. He didn't have time for this.

If he couldn't get one of these dinosaurs to the landing site, they would never get out of there — or worse, the mother T. rex would catch up to Jeff and Shannon. Or even worse yet —

ROOOOOARRRRRRRR!

The mother T. rex would give up chasing Shannon and Jeff and come back to check on her kids.

Mike was trapped.

He was caught between the mother T. rex and her four babies with nowhere to run. There was too much open field to try to reach the safety of any trees. This was not good.

Behind the lumbering mother T. rex, Mike could see Shannon and Jeff emerge from out of the forest. They wouldn't be able to do anything to help him.

The mother came closer and closer until Mike could feel hot breath shoot from her nostrils. Mike was frozen with fear until the mother T. rex nudged him ever so gently with the tip of her snout.

Mike didn't understand what was
happening. The mother nudged him
again, but a bit harder this time as she
snorted. Now the baby T. rex got in on
the action. They were all over Mike,
carefully tugging at his clothes and
pushing him this way and that.

Dino-Mike realized that they were playing with him. They were treating him as if he was one of the family.

Jeff and Shannon came closer but kept enough distance so that the mother did not react.

"W-what's happening?" asked Mike.

"How cute," said Shannon. "They must remember you from before. They probably imprinted on you. You were the first thing they had contact with, so they feel close to you."

"We've seen stuff like this happen before, like dinosaurs become friendly with their keepers," said Jeff.

"I think they like you," said Shannon, giggling a bit.

"What do we do now?" asked Jeff.

Mike looked at the leash dangling from the neck of one of the baby dinosaurs and slowly reached for it. Having gotten it without incident, he started to lead the dinosaur.

"Follow me, but keep your distance," he said to Shannon and Jeff.

Sure enough, the entire family went with him. They would run ahead or bump Mike playfully through the course of the entire walk. The mother T. rex followed right on their heels.

Mike led them all the way to the landing site. Within feet of the spot where Mike landed, the mother T. rex stopped. She wouldn't go any farther.

"What's the matter with her?" asked Mike.

"She remembers this spot," said Jeff. "She remembers what it was like to go through the time portal the first time, and she didn't like it."

"Well, what do we do now?" asked Shannon.

Mike looked behind him and saw the four baby T. rex being their usual playful selves, but they were glowing!

"THEY'RE GLOWING!" said Mike.

Dino-Mike knew what this meant. It meant that they were — But how? They never went forward in time . . . because they were unhatched.

"They were unhatched, but technically they did go forward! They were carried by the mother! It's basic biology!" Mike exclaimed.

"That's right! They're activating the time portal!" said Jeff.

"They're getting glowier." Mike knew that wasn't a real word the minute he said it, but it was true, they were glowing brighter.

"We need to get closer," said Jeff, standing far enough away with Shannon to not anger the T. rex.

"Wait," said Mike as he slowly approached the mother T. rex.

Dino-Mike put his hand up. As if the mother T. rex knew, she pushed the top of her head into Mike's hand.

"Okay," said Mike.

Jeff and Shannon slowly moved past the mother T. rex and behind Mike. Mike patted the mother on the head and then moved back to stand with Jeff and Shannon and the four young T. rex. The air crackled around them, and the T. rex glowed brighter.

"You might want to call your babies home, Samantha," said Mike to the mother T. rex.

The mother let out a snort and a low rumbling bellow. The four kids quickly left Mike's side and ran to their mother.

The air swirled around Mike, Shannon, and Jeff.

"Thanks," said Mike to the mother T. rex.

Moments later, the group disappeared into thin air, leaving the four baby T. rex looking confused.

Chapter 10

UNDERWATER AGAIN

"It worked!"

Mike didn't think he could be any happier to see Shannon's underwater home and dino sanctuary. They were standing in the time portal room, where Mike had made his journey to the past.

"Ha!" said Jeff! "I'll be darned if you weren't right on the money, Mike!"

"I'm so glad to be safely back home!" exclaimed Shannon.

"Your father knows we left, but will anyone else wonder where we've been?" asked Mike.

"Don't worry about *your* father. To him and everyone else, only a few minutes have gone by since we left," explained Shannon as they walked down the long corridor.

"That's a relief," said Mike. "I didn't get much information from your father about how this worked before I left."

Right on cue, Dr. Broome and Mike's father came around the corner.

"Son, where is your jacket?" said Mike's father.

"Oh, um, Dad, I think I . . ."

"Here's your jacket, Mike," said Dr. Broome, holding a Dino Jacket. "You must have left it in the dock area."

Mike was confused. This couldn't be his jacket. The one his dad gave him was gone. *How is this possible?* he thought.

"Uh, thanks," was all he could muster.

"Funny thing," said Mike's dad. "Did I ever tell you that Dr. Broome is, in fact, the one who designed the Dino Jacket?"

Mike was shocked. It all started to make sense. Dr. Broome had filled the Dino Jacket with all those cool dinosaur-type gadgets. That's why Mike's father didn't know about so many of them.

"Wow. Thanks, Dr. Broome!" Mike exclaimed.

"Not a problem, Mike. Just make sure you keep it in a safe place. I put a few extra features in there for you to explore." Dr. Broome smiled and winked at him.

Dr. Broome then turned to Mike's dad and said, "You know something, Dr. Evans? I like you, and I think we have a great working relationship. Plus the kids get along so well together. How would you like a job here with me?"

"I don't know what to say," said Mike's dad.

"Why don't we go back to my office and discuss," Dr. Broome offered.

As the adults left, the kids all stayed behind. Mike held the jacket out and stared at it. It was exactly like the other one. He wondered what new secrets were hidden inside. He couldn't help but smile.

Jeff stepped forward. "I have to admit, you really helped us out, Mike. I want to apologize for all the mean things I did. From now on, I'm on the good side of things," he said. "Well, I better go clean my room before I get grounded again."

Jeff turned to go, but then looked back at Mike again.

"You're okay in my book, Dino-Mike, and you're welcome at our home any time," said Jurassic Jeff.

Mike smiled at Shannon. It had been a wild and crazy set of adventures from the minute he met both Shannon and Jeff, but he was happy to have made such good friends.

"You seem pretty happy," said Shannon. "Go ahead. Put it on."

Mike put on the Dino Jacket. He pulled the hood with the T. rex face over his head.

ROOOOAAAAAAARRRR!

The familiar T. rex roar sounded and the bright lights of the eyes flashed on. It felt right.

Mike took the hood down. "I wonder if this one has all of the same gadgets as the last one."

"Knowing my dad, yes. All of them and probably a few you have yet to discover." Shannon laughed.

"This looks like a newer model," Shannon continued. "It probably has a portal key in there with a Return Remote. He's been working on perfecting how to control the time travel."

"Really?" said a shocked Mike. "You think so? I'll still be able to go to the Cretaceous period?"

"The portal doesn't just go to one time period," explained Shannon.

"So it can go anywhere in the past?" said an even more excited Mike.

"No . . . not just the past. It can go ANYWHERE," she said.

"You mean —?" Mike began.

Shannon put her hands up in the air as if showing Mike the imaginary stars in the sky. "Do you remember the planetarium in New York? What if you could go to the moon or the stars, or better yet, to different planets . . . ones that aren't even in our solar system?"

Mike was stunned as he thought about her imaginary scenario. Shannon smiled and walked away.

Mike looked down at his Dino Jacket, and it began to glow slightly. A smile came across his face.

Time for another adventure! thought Dino-Mike.

GLOSSARY

Jurassic Period (juh-RA-sik PIHR-ee-uhd)—a period of time about 200 to 144 million years ago

paleontologist (pale-ee-uhn-TOL-uh-gist)—a scientist who deals with fossils and other life-forms

pterodactyl (ter-uh-DAK-til)—a prehistoric flying reptile with large wings supported by very large fourth fingers

triceratops (try-SER-uh-tops)—a large, plant-eating dinosaur with three horns and a fan-shaped collar of bone

tyrannosaurus (ti-RAN-uh-sor-uhs)—a large, meat-eating dinosaur that walked on its hind legs, also known as a T. rex

DINO FACTS!

What does the word "dinosaur" mean? The word comes from the Greek language and means "terrible lizard." In 1842, paleontologist Richard Owen was the first person to call dinosaurs by this name.

The world's tallest dinosaur fossil is displayed at Museum für Naturkunde, Berlin's natural history museum. The Brachiosaurus stands 41 feet, 5 inches high.

Tyrannosaurus rex lived between 65 to 145 million years ago during a time known as the Cretaceous period (kri-TAY-shuss PIHR-ee-uhd).

The T. rex's arms were surprisingly small. At only 3 feet long, they were too short to capture prey. Instead of grabbing prey with its tiny arms, T. rex grabbed food with its teeth. Each T. rex tooth measured more than 9 inches long!

T. rex used its giant teeth to satisfy a giant appetite. Scientists believe that with one bite the T. rex could gobble up about 500 pounds of meat.

All of the T. rex fossils discovered have been found in North America. In 1990, one of the best-known and most complete skeletons was discovered in South Dakota by fossil hunter Sue Hendrickson. The fossil, known simply as "Sue," is now on display at the Field Museum in Chicago.

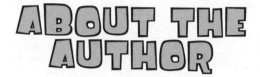

ABOUT THE AUTHOR

Bronx, New York-born writer and artist Franco Aureliani has been drawing comics since he could hold a crayon. Currently residing in upstate New York with his wife, Ivette, and son, Nicolas, he spends most of his days in his Batcave-like studio where he works on comics projects. In 1995, Franco founded Blindwolf Studios, an independent art studio where he and fellow creators can create children's comics. Franco is the creator, artist, and writer of Weirdsville, L'il Creeps, and Eagle All Star, as well as the cocreator and writer of Patrick the Wolf Boy.

Franco recently finished work on Superman Family Adventures, and is now cowriting the series The Green Team: Teen Trillionaires and Tiny Titans by DC Comics. When he's not writing and drawing, Franco teaches high school art.